Dear Parent:

Congratulations! Your child is taking the first steps on an exciting journey. The destination? Independent reading!

STEP INTO READING® will help your child get there. The program offers five steps to reading success. Each step includes fun stories and colorful art. There are also Step into Reading Sticker Books, Step into Reading Math Readers, Step into Reading Phonics Readers, Step into Reading Write-In Readers, and Step into Reading Phonics Boxed Sets—a complete literacy program with something for every child.

Learning to Read, Step by Step!

Ready to Read Preschool–Kindergarten
• big type and easy words • rhyme and rhythm • picture clues
For children who know the alphabet and are eager to begin reading.

Reading with Help Preschool–Grade 1
• basic vocabulary • short sentences • simple stories
For children who recognize familiar words and sound out new words with help.

Reading on Your Own Grades 1–3
• engaging characters • easy-to-follow plots • popular topics
For children who are ready to read on their own.

Reading Paragraphs Grades 2–3
• challenging vocabulary • short paragraphs • exciting stories
For newly independent readers who read simple sentences with confidence.

Ready for Chapters Grades 2–4
• chapters • longer paragraphs • full-color art
For children who want to take the plunge into chapter books but still like colorful pictures.

STEP INTO READING® is designed to give every child a successful reading experience. The grade levels are only guides. Children can progress through the steps at their own speed, developing confidence in their reading, no matter what their grade.

Remember, a lifetime love of reading starts with a single step!

Special thanks to Diane Reichenberger, Cindy Ledermann, Jocelyn Morgan, Tanya Mann, Julia Phelps, Sharon Woloszyk, Rita Lichtwardt, Carla Alford, Renee Reeser Zelnick, Rob Hudnut, David Wiebe, Shelley Dvi-Vardhana, Gabrielle Miles, Rainmaker Entertainment, Walter P. Martishius, and Sarah Lazar.

Visit us on the Web!
StepIntoReading.com
randomhouse.com/kids

Educators and librarians, for a variety of teaching tools, visit us at RHTeachersLibrarians.com

ISBN 978-0-385-37307-4 (trade) — ISBN 978-0-375-97192-1 (lib. bdg.)

Printed in the United States of America   10 9 8 7 6 5 4 3 2 1

Barbie™
The Pearl
Princess

Pretty Pearl
MERMAID

Adapted by Jennifer Liberts Weinberg

Based on the screenplay by
Cydne Clark & Steve Granat

Illustrated by Ulkutay Design Group

Random House 🏠 New York

The mermaid king
and queen have a baby.
One day she will
rule the kingdom.

The mermaid princess
has magical powers.
She makes pearls
dance and glow!

Caligo is the king's
evil brother.
Caligo wants his son,
Fergis, to be king.

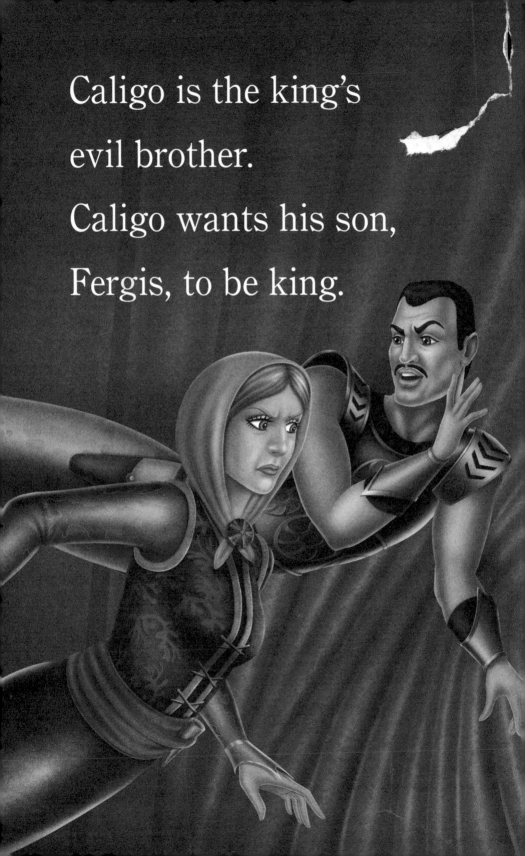

He asks an old mermaid
named Scylla
to get rid of
the princess.

Scylla falls in love
with the baby.
She vows
to keep the princess
safe from Caligo.

Scylla hides
the mermaid princess
in a sea cave.
She names her Lumina
and raises her.
Lumina does not know
she is a princess.

Lumina's best friend
is a pink sea horse
named Kuda.
The friends pretend to be
princesses.

12

Lumina makes pearls
shimmer and sparkle!

13

The king and queen miss Lumina. Caligo wants his son to be the next ruler.

Caligo orders Murray the eel to bring Scylla a message.

Murray tells Scylla to go to the royal ball and poison the king. He gives her an invitation.

If she doesn't obey,
Caligo will tell everyone
she took the princess.

Lumina wants to go
to the royal ball, too.
Scylla says no.

Scylla forgot
the invitation.

Lumina and Kuda will
bring it to Scylla
at the palace.

Lumina and Kuda meet
a scary fish named Spike.
Lumina covers his spikes
with magic pearls.
Now he is friendly!

They reach the kingdom.
Lumina makes friends
in a beauty salon.

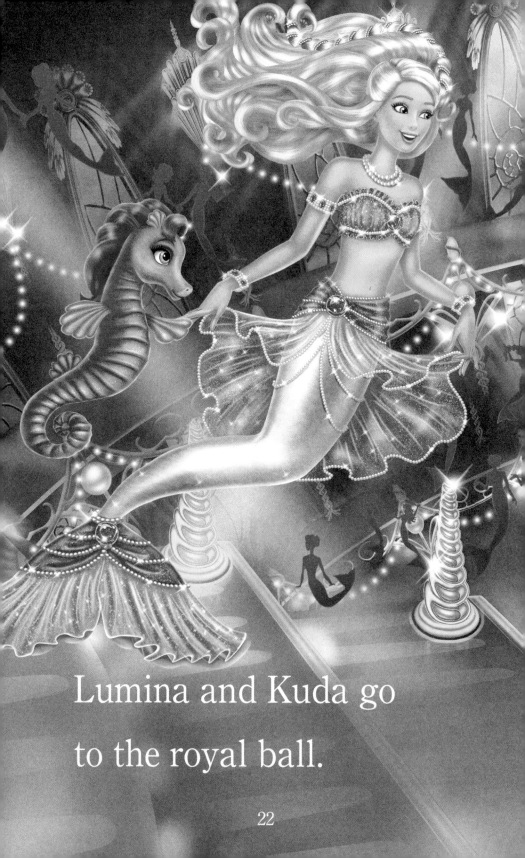

Lumina and Kuda go
to the royal ball.

Lumina wears a pink gown
covered in pearls.

Lumina overhears
Caligo's evil plan.

She tries
to stop him
and help Scylla.

Scylla tries
to tell the king
the truth about Caligo.
Caligo wants to stop her.

He pushes Scylla
onto a spike!
Scylla is hurt.

Caligo's guards try
to stop Lumina.
Lumina protects Scylla
with swirling pearls.

Fergis has flowers
that can save Scylla!
He gives Scylla
the flower petals.

The king sees
Lumina's pearl magic.
He knows Lumina must be
his daughter!

The king gives Lumina
the Pearl of the Sea.
Her dress and pearls
glitter and glow!

Lumina is the magical
mermaid princess!
Scylla is saved.
The mermaid kingdom
is full of joy!